A Visit to Three Fronts

By
Arthur Conan Doyle

A GLIMPSE OF THE BRITISH ARMY

I

It is not an easy matter to write from the front. You know that there are several courteous but inexorable gentlemen who may have a word in the matter, and their presence 'imparts but small ease to the style.' But above all you have the twin censors of your own conscience and common sense, which assure you that, if all other readers fail you, you will certainly find a most attentive one in the neighbourhood of the Haupt-Quartier. An instructive story is still told of how a certain well-meaning traveller recorded his satisfaction with the appearance of the big guns at the retiring and peaceful village of Jamais, and how three days later, by an interesting coincidence, the village of Jamais passed suddenly off the map and dematerialised into brickdust and splinters.

I have been with soldiers on the warpath before, but never have I had a day so crammed with experiences and impressions as yesterday. Some of them at least I can faintly convey to the reader, and if they ever reach the eye of that gentleman at the Haupt-Quartier they will give him little joy. For the crowning impression of all is the enormous imperturbable confidence of the Army and its extraordinary efficiency in organisation, administration, material, and personnel. I met in one day a sample of many types, an Army commander, a corps commander, two divisional commanders, staff officers of many grades, and, above all, I met repeatedly the two very great men whom Britain has produced, the private soldier and the regimental officer. Everywhere and on every face one read the same spirit of cheerful bravery. Even the half-mad cranks whose absurd consciences prevent them from barring the way to the devil seemed to me to be turning into men under the prevailing influence. I saw a batch of them, neurotic and largely be-spectacled, but working with a will by the roadside. They will volunteer for the trenches yet.

If there are pessimists among us they are not to be found among the men who are doing the work. There is no foolish bravado, no under-rating of a dour opponent, but there is a quick, alert, confident attention to the job in hand which is an inspiration to the observer. These brave lads are guarding Britain in the present. See to it that Britain guards them in the future! We have a bad record in this matter. It must be changed. They are the wards of the nation, both officers and men. Socialism has never had an attraction for me, but I should be a Socialist to-morrow if I thought that to ease a tax on wealth these men should ever suffer for the time or health that they gave to the public cause.

'Get out of the car. Don't let it stay here. It may be hit.' These words from a staff officer give you the first idea that things are going to happen. Up to then you might have been driving through the black country in the Walsall district with the population of Aldershot let loose upon its dingy roads. 'Put on this shrapnel helmet. That hat of yours would infuriate the Boche'—this was an unkind allusion to the only uniform which I have a right to wear. 'Take this gas helmet. You won't need it, but it is a standing order. Now come on!'

We cross a meadow and enter a trench. Here and there it comes to the surface again where there is dead ground. At one such point an old church stands, with an unexploded shell sticking out of the wall. A century hence folk will journey to see that shell. Then on again through an endless cutting. It is slippery clay below. I have no nails in my boots, an iron pot on my head, and the sun above me. I will remember that walk. Ten telephone wires run down the side. Here and there large thistles and other plants grow from the clay walls, so immobile have been our lines. Occasionally there are patches of untidiness. 'Shells,' says the officer laconically. There is a racket of guns before us and behind, especially behind, but danger seems remote with all these Bairnfather groups of cheerful Tommies at work around us. I pass one group of grimy, tattered boys. A glance at their shoulders shows me that they are of a public school battalion. 'I thought you fellows were all officers now,' I remarked. 'No, sir, we like it better so.' 'Well, it will be a great memory for you. We are all in your debt.'

They salute, and we squeeze past them. They had the fresh, brown faces of boy cricketers. But their comrades were men of a different type, with hard, strong, rugged features, and the eyes of men who have seen strange sights. These are veterans, men of Mons, and their young pals of the public schools have something to live up to.

Up to this we have only had two clay walls to look at. But now our interminable and tropical walk is lightened by the sight of a British aeroplane sailing overhead. Numerous shrapnel bursts are all round it, but she floats on serenely, a thing of delicate beauty against the blue background. Now another passes—and yet another. All morning we saw them circling and swooping, and never a sign of a Boche. They tell me it is nearly always so—that we hold the air, and that the Boche intruder, save at early morning, is a rare bird. A visit to the line would reassure Mr. Pemberton-Billing. 'We have never met a British aeroplane which was not ready to fight,' said a captured German aviator the other day. There is a fine stern courtesy between the airmen on either side, each dropping notes into the other's aerodromes to tell the fate of missing officers. Had the whole war been fought by the Germans as their airmen have conducted it (I do not speak of course of the Zeppelin murderers), a peace would eventually have been more easily arranged. As it is, if every frontier could be settled, it would be a hard thing to stop until all that is associated with the words Cavell, Zeppelin, Wittenberg, Lusitania, and Louvain has been brought to the bar of the world's Justice.

And now we are there—in what is surely the most wonderful spot in the world, the front firing trench, the outer breakwater which holds back the German tide. How strange that this monstrous oscillation of giant forces, setting in from east to west, should find their equilibrium here across this particular meadow of Flanders. 'How far?' I ask. '180 yards,' says my guide. 'Pop!' remarks a third person just in front. 'A sniper,' says my guide; 'take a look through the periscope.' I do so. There is some rusty wire before me, then a field sloping slightly upwards with knee-deep grass, then rusty wire again, and a red line of broken earth. There is not a sign of movement, but sharp eyes are always watching us, even as these crouching soldiers around me are watching them. There are dead Germans in the grass before us. You need not see them to know that they are there. A wounded soldier sits in a corner nursing his leg. Here and there men pop out like rabbits from dug-outs and mine-shafts. Others sit on the fire-step or lean smoking against the clay wall. Who would dream to look at their bold, careless faces that this is a front line, and that at any moment it is possible that a grey wave may submerge them? With all their careless bearing I notice that every man has his gas helmet and his rifle within easy reach.

A mile of front trenches and then we are on our way back down that weary walk. Then I am whisked off upon a ten mile drive. There is a pause for lunch at Corps Headquarters, and after it we are taken to a medal presentation in a market square. Generals Munro, Haking and Landon, famous fighting soldiers all three, are the British representatives. Munro with a ruddy face, and brain above all bulldog below; Haking, pale, distinguished, intellectual; Landon a pleasant, genial country squire. An elderly French General stands beside them.

British infantry keep the ground. In front are about fifty Frenchmen in civil dress of every grade of life, workmen and gentlemen, in a double rank. They are all so wounded that they are back in civil life, but to-day they are to have some solace for their wounds. They lean heavily on sticks, their bodies are twisted and maimed, but their faces are shining with pride and joy. The French General draws his sword and addresses them. One catches words like 'honneur' and 'patrie.' They lean forward on their crutches, hanging on every syllable which comes hissing and rasping from under that heavy white moustache. Then the medals are pinned on. One poor lad is terribly wounded and needs two sticks. A little girl runs out with some flowers. He leans forward and tries to kiss her, but the crutches slip and he nearly falls upon her. It was a pitiful but beautiful little scene.

Now the British candidates march up one by one for their medals, hale, hearty men, brown and fit. There is a smart young officer of Scottish Rifles; and then a selection of Worcesters, Welsh Fusiliers and Scots Fusiliers, with one funny little Highlander, a tiny figure with a soup-bowl helmet, a grinning boy's face beneath it, and a bedraggled uniform. 'Many acts of great bravery'—such was the record for which he was decorated. Even the French wounded smiled at his quaint appearance, as they did at another Briton who had acquired the chewing-gum habit, and came up for his medal as if he had been called suddenly in the middle of his dinner, which he was still endeavouring to bolt. Then came the end, with the National Anthem. The British regiment formed fours and went past. To me that was the most impressive sight of any. They were the Queen's West Surreys, a veteran regiment of the great Ypres battle. What grand fellows! As the order came 'Eyes right,' and all those fierce, dark faces flashed round about us, I felt the might of the British infantry, the intense individuality which is not incompatible with the highest discipline. Much they had endured, but a great spirit shone from their faces. I confess that as I looked at those brave English lads, and thought of what we owe to them and to their like who have passed on, I felt more emotional than befits a Briton in foreign parts.

Now the ceremony was ended, and once again we set out for the front. It was to an artillery observation post that we were bound, and once again my description must be bounded by discretion. Suffice it, that in an hour I found myself, together with a razor-keen young artillery observer and an excellent old sportsman of a Russian prince, jammed into a very small space, and staring through a slit at the German lines. In front of us lay a vast plain, scarred and slashed, with bare places at intervals, such as you see where gravel pits break a green common. Not a sign of life or movement, save some wheeling crows. And yet down there, within a mile or so, is the population of a city. Far away a single train is puffing at the back of the German lines. We are here on a definite errand. Away to the right, nearly three miles off, is a small red house, dim to the eye but clear in the glasses, which is suspected as a German post. It is to go up this afternoon. The gun is some distance away, but I hear the telephone directions. '"Mother" will soon do her in,' remarks the gunner boy cheerfully. 'Mother' is the name of the gun. 'Give her five six three four,' he cries through the 'phone. 'Mother' utters a horrible bellow from somewhere on our right. An enormous spout of smoke rises ten seconds later from near the house. 'A little short,' says our gunner. 'Two and a half minutes left,' adds a little small voice, which represents another observer at a different angle. 'Raise her seven five,' says our boy encouragingly. 'Mother' roars more angrily than ever. 'How will that do?' she seems to say. 'One and a half right,' says our invisible gossip. I wonder how the folk in the house are feeling as the shells creep ever nearer. 'Gun laid, sir,' says the telephone. 'Fire!' I am looking through my glass. A flash of fire on the house, a huge pillar of dust and smoke —then it settles, and an unbroken field is there. The German post has gone up. 'It's a dear little gun,' says the officer boy. 'And her shells are reliable,' remarked a senior behind us. 'They vary with different calibres, but "Mother" never goes wrong.' The German line was very quiet. 'Pourquoi ils ne répondent pas?' asked the Russian prince. 'Yes, they are quiet to-day,' answered the senior. 'But we get it in the neck sometimes.' We are all led off to be introduced to 'Mother,' who sits, squat and black, amid twenty of her grimy children who wait upon and feed her. She is an important person is 'Mother,' and her importance grows. It gets clearer with every month that it is she, and only she, who can lead us to the Rhine. She can and she will if the factories of Britain can beat those of the Hun. See to it, you working men and women of Britain. Work now if you rest for ever after, for the fate of Europe and of all that is dear to us is in your hands. For 'Mother' is a dainty eater, and needs good food and plenty. She is fond of strange lodgings, too, in which she prefers safety to dignity. But that is a dangerous subject.

One more experience of this wonderful day—the most crowded with impressions of my whole life. At night we take a car and drive north, and ever north, until at a late hour we halt and climb a hill in the darkness. Below is a wonderful sight. Down on the flats, in a huge semi-circle, lights are rising and falling. They are very brilliant, going up for a few seconds and then dying down. Sometimes a dozen are in the air at one time. There are the dull thuds of explosions and an occasional rat-tat-tat. I have seen nothing like it, but the nearest comparison would be an enormous ten-mile railway station in full swing at night, with signals winking, lamps waving, engines hissing and carriages bumping. It is a terrible place down yonder, a place which will live as long as military history is written, for it is the Ypres Salient. What a salient it is, too! A huge curve, as outlined by the lights, needing only a little more to be an encirclement. Something caught the rope as it closed, and that something was the British soldier. But it is a perilous place still by day and by night. Never shall I forget the impression of ceaseless, malignant activity which was borne in upon me by the white, winking lights, the red sudden glares, and the horrible thudding noises in that place of death beneath me.

II

In old days we had a great name as organisers. Then came a long period when we deliberately adopted a policy of individuality and 'go as you please.' Now once again in our sore need we have called on all our power of administration and direction. But it has not deserted us. We still have it in a supreme degree. Even in peace time we have shown it in that vast, well-oiled, swift-running, noiseless machine called the British Navy. But now our powers have risen with the need of them. The expansion of the Navy has been a miracle, the management of the transport a greater one, the formation of the new Army the greatest of all time. To get the men was the least of the difficulties. To put them here, with everything down to the lid of the last field saucepan in its place, that is the marvel. The tools of the gunners, and of the sappers, to say nothing of the knowledge of how to use them, are in themselves a huge problem. But it has all been met and mastered, and will be to the end. But don't let us talk any more about the muddling of the War Office. It has become just a little ridiculous.

I have told of my first day, when I visited the front trenches, saw the work of 'Mother,' and finally that marvellous spectacle, the Ypres Salient at night. I have passed the night at the headquarters of a divisional-general, Capper, who might truly be called one of the two fathers of the British flying force, for it was he, with Templer, who laid the first foundations from which so great an organisation has arisen. My morning was spent in visiting two fighting brigadiers, cheery weather-beaten soldiers, respectful, as all our soldiers are, of the prowess of the Hun, but serenely confident that we can beat him. In company with one of them I ascended a hill, the reverse slope of which was swarming with cheerful infantry in every stage of dishabille, for they were cleaning up after the trenches. Once over the slope we advanced with some care, and finally reached a certain spot from which we looked down upon the German line. It was the advanced observation post, about a thousand yards from the German trenches, with our own trenches between us. We could see the two lines, sometimes only a few yards, as it seemed, apart, extending for miles on either side. The sinister silence and solitude were strangely dramatic. Such vast crowds of men, such intensity of feeling, and yet only that open rolling countryside, with never a movement in its whole expanse.

The afternoon saw us in the Square at Ypres. It is the city of a dream, this modern Pompeii, destroyed, deserted and desecrated, but with a sad, proud dignity which made you involuntarily lower your voice as you passed through the ruined streets. It is a more considerable place than I had imagined, with many traces of ancient grandeur. No words can describe the absolute splintered wreck that the Huns have made of it. The effect of some of the shells has been grotesque. One boiler-plated water-tower, a thing forty or fifty feet high, was actually standing on its head like a great metal top. There is not a living soul in the place save a few pickets of soldiers, and a number of cats which become fierce and dangerous. Now and then a shell still falls, but the Huns probably know that the devastation is already complete.

We stood in the lonely grass-grown Square, once the busy centre of the town, and we marvelled at the beauty of the smashed cathedral and the tottering Cloth Hall beside it. Surely at their best they could not have looked more wonderful than now. If they were preserved even so, and if a heaven-inspired artist were to model a statue of Belgium in front, Belgium with one hand pointing to the treaty by which Prussia guaranteed her safety and the other to the sacrilege behind her, it would make the most impressive group in the world. It was an evil day for Belgium when her frontier was violated, but it was a worse one for Germany. I venture to prophesy that it will be regarded by history as the greatest military as well as political error that has ever been made. Had the great guns that destroyed Liége made their first breach at Verdun, what chance was there for Paris? Those few weeks of warning and preparation saved France, and left Germany as she now is, like a weary and furious bull, tethered fast in the place of trespass and waiting for the inevitable pole-axe.

We were glad to get out of the place, for the gloom of it lay as heavy upon our hearts as the shrapnel helmets did upon our heads. Both were lightened as we sped back past empty and shattered villas to where, just behind the danger line, the normal life of rural Flanders was carrying on as usual. A merry sight helped to cheer us, for scudding down wind above our heads came a Boche aeroplane, with two British at her tail barking away with their machine guns, like two swift terriers after a cat. They shot rat-tat-tatting across the sky until we lost sight of them in the heat haze over the German line.

The afternoon saw us on the Sharpenburg, from which many a million will gaze in days to come, for from no other point can so much be seen. It is a spot forbid, but a special permit took us up, and the sentry on duty, having satisfied himself of our bona fides, proceeded to tell us tales of the war in a pure Hull dialect which might have been Chinese for all that I could understand. That he was a 'terrier' and had nine children were the only facts I could lay hold of. But I wished to be silent and to think—even, perhaps, to pray. Here, just below my feet, were the spots which our dear lads, three of them my own kith, have sanctified with their blood. Here, fighting for the freedom of the world, they cheerily gave their all. On that sloping meadow to the left of the row of houses on the opposite ridge the London Scottish fought to the death on that grim November morning when the Bavarians reeled back from their shot-torn line. That plain away on the other side of Ypres was the place where the three grand Canadian brigades, first of all men, stood up to the damnable cowardly gases of the Hun. Down yonder is Hill 60, that blood-soaked kopje. The ridge over the fields was held by the cavalry against two army corps, and there where the sun strikes the red roof among the trees I can just see Gheluveld, a name for ever to be associated with Haig and the most vital battle of the war. As I turn away I am faced by my Hull Territorial, who still says incomprehensible things. I look at him with other eyes. He has fought on yonder plain. He has slain Huns, and he has nine children. Could any one better epitomise the duties of a good citizen? I could have found it in my heart to salute him had I not known that it would have shocked him and made him unhappy.

It has been a full day, and the next is even fuller, for it is my privilege to lunch at Headquarters, and to make the acquaintance of the Commander-in-chief and of his staff. It would be an invasion of private hospitality if I were to give the public the impressions which I carried from that charming château. I am the more sorry, since they were very vivid and strong. This much I will say—and any man who is a face reader will not need to have it said—that if the Army stands still it is not by the will of its commander. There will, I swear, be no happier man in Europe when the day has come and the hour. It is human to err, but never possibly can some types err by being backward. We have a superb army in France. It needs the right leader to handle it. I came away happier and more confident than ever as to the future.

Extraordinary are the contrasts of war. Within three hours of leaving the quiet atmosphere of the Headquarters Château I was present at what in any other war would have been looked upon as a brisk engagement. As it was it would certainly figure in one of our desiccated reports as an activity of the artillery. The noise as we struck the line at this new point showed that the matter was serious, and, indeed, we had chosen the spot because it had been the storm centre of the last week. The method of approach chosen by our experienced guide was in itself a tribute to the gravity of the affair. As one comes from the settled order of Flanders into the actual scene of war, the first sign of it is one of the stationary, sausage-shaped balloons, a chain of which marks the ring in which the great wrestlers are locked. We pass under this, ascend a hill, and find ourselves in a garden where for a year no feet save those of wanderers like ourselves have stood. There is a wild, confused luxuriance of growth more beautiful to my eye than anything which the care of man can produce. One old shell-hole of vast diameter has filled itself with forget-me-nots, and appears as a graceful basin of light blue flowers, held up as an atonement to heaven for the brutalities of man. Through the tangled bushes we creep, then across a yard—'Please stoop and run as you pass this point'—and finally to a small opening in a wall, whence the battle lies not so much before as beside us. For a moment we have a front seat at the great world-drama, God's own problem play, working surely to its magnificent end. One feels a sort of shame to crouch here in comfort, a useless spectator, while brave men down yonder are facing that pelting shower of iron.

There is a large field on our left rear, and the German gunners have the idea that there is a concealed battery therein. They are systematically searching for it. A great shell explodes in the top corner, but gets nothing more solid than a few tons of clay. You can read the mind of Gunner Fritz. 'Try the lower corner!' says he, and up goes the earth-cloud once again. 'Perhaps it's hid about the middle. I'll try.' Earth again, and nothing more. 'I believe I was right the first time after all,' says hopeful Fritz. So another shell comes into the top corner. The field is as full of pits as a Gruyère cheese, but Fritz gets nothing by his perseverance. Perhaps there never was a battery there at all. One effect he obviously did attain. He made several other British batteries exceedingly angry. 'Stop that tickling, Fritz!' was the burden of their cry. Where they were we could no more see than Fritz could, but their constant work was very clear along the German line. We appeared to be using more shrapnel and the Germans more high explosives, but that may have been just the chance of the day. The Vimy Ridge was on our right, and before us was the old French position, with the labyrinth of terrible memories and the long hill of Lorette. When, last year, the French, in a three weeks' battle, fought their way up that hill, it was an exhibition of sustained courage which even their military annals can seldom have beaten.

And so I turn from the British line. Another and more distant task lies before me. I come away with the deep sense of the difficult task which lies before the Army, but with a deeper one of the ability of these men to do all that soldiers can ever be asked to perform. Let the guns clear the way for the infantry, and the rest will follow. It all lies with the guns. But the guns, in turn, depend upon our splendid workers at home, who, men and women, are doing so grandly. Let them not be judged by a tiny minority, who are given, perhaps, too much attention in our journals. We have all made sacrifices in the war, but when the full story comes to be told, perhaps the greatest sacrifice of all is that which Labour made when, with a sigh, she laid aside that which it had taken so many weary years to build.

A GLIMPSE OF THE ITALIAN ARMY

One meets with such extreme kindness and consideration among the Italians that there is a real danger lest one's personal feeling of obligation should warp one's judgment or hamper one's expression. Making every possible allowance for this, I come away from them, after a very wide if superficial view of all that they are doing, with a deep feeling of admiration and a conviction that no army in the world could have made a braver attempt to advance under conditions of extraordinary difficulty.

First a word as to the Italian soldier. He is a type by himself which differs from the earnest solidarity of the new French army, and from the businesslike alertness of the Briton, and yet has a very special dash and fire of its own, covered over by a very pleasing and unassuming manner. London has not yet forgotten Durando of Marathon fame. He was just such another easy smiling youth as I now see everywhere around me. Yet there came a day when a hundred thousand Londoners hung upon his every movement—when strong men gasped and women wept at his invincible but unavailing spirit. When he had fallen senseless in that historic race on the very threshold of his goal, so high was the determination within him, that while he floundered on the track like a broken-backed horse, with the senses gone out of him, his legs still continued to drum upon the cinder path. Then when by pure will power he staggered to his feet and drove his dazed body across the line, it was an exhibition of pluck which put the little sunburned baker straightway among London's heroes. Durando's spirit is alive to-day, I see thousands of him all around me. A thousand such, led by a few young gentlemen of the type who occasionally give us object lessons in how to ride at Olympia, make no mean battalion. It has been a war of most desperate ventures, but never once has there been a lack of volunteers. The Tyrolese are good men—too good to be fighting in so rotten a cause. But from first to last the Alpini have had the ascendency in the hill fighting, as the line regiments have against the Kaiserlics upon the plain. Caesar told how the big Germans used to laugh at his little men until they had been at handgrips with them. The Austrians could tell the same tale. The spirit in the ranks is something marvellous. There have been occasions when every officer has fallen and yet the men have pushed on, have taken a position and then waited for official directions.

But if that is so, you will ask, why is it that they have not made more impression upon the enemy's position? The answer lies in the strategical position of Italy, and it can be discussed without any technicalities. A child could understand it. The Alps form such a bar across the north that there are only two points where serious operations are possible. One is the Trentino Salient where Austria can always threaten and invade Italy. She lies in the mountains with the plains beneath her. She can always invade the plain, but the Italians cannot seriously invade the mountains, since the passes would only lead to other mountains beyond. Therefore their only possible policy is to hold the Austrians back. This they have most successfully done, and though the Austrians with the aid of a shattering heavy artillery have recently made some advance, it is perfectly certain that they can never really carry out any serious invasion. The Italians then have done all that could be done in this quarter. There remains the other front, the opening by the sea. Here the Italians had a chance to advance over a front of plain bounded by a river with hills beyond. They cleared the plain, they crossed the river, they fought a battle very like our own battle of the Aisne upon the slopes of the hills, taking 20,000 Austrian prisoners, and now they are faced by barbed wire, machine guns, cemented trenches, and every other device which has held them as it has held every one else. But remember what they have done for the common cause and be grateful for it. They have in a year occupied some forty Austrian divisions, and relieved our Russian allies to that very appreciable extent. They have killed or wounded a quarter of a million, taken 40,000, and drawn to themselves a large portion of the artillery. That is their record up to date. As to the future it is very easy to prophesy. They will continue to absorb large enemy armies. Neither side can advance far as matters stand. But if the Russians advance and Austria has to draw her men to the East, there will be a tiger spring for Trieste. If manhood can break the line, then I believe the Durandos will do it.

'Trieste o morte!' I saw chalked upon the walls all over North Italy.

That is the Italian objective.

And they are excellently led. Cadorna is an old Roman, a man cast in the big simple mould of antiquity, frugal in his tastes, clear in his aims, with no thought outside his duty. Every one loves and trusts him. Porro, the Chief of the Staff, who was good enough to explain the strategical position to me, struck me as a man of great clearness of vision, middle-sized, straight as a dart, with an eagle face grained and coloured like an old walnut. The whole of the staff work is, as experts assure me, moot excellently done.

So much for the general situation. Let me descend for a moment to my own trivial adventures since leaving the British front. Of France I hope to say more in the future, and so I will pass at a bound to Padua, where it appeared that the Austrian front had politely advanced to meet me, for I was wakened betimes in the morning by the dropping of bombs, the rattle of anti-aircraft guns, and the distant rat-tat-tat of a maxim high up in the air. I heard when I came down later that the intruder had been driven away and that little damage had been done. The work of the Austrian aeroplanes is, however, very aggressive behind the Italian lines, for they have the great advantage that a row of fine cities lies at their mercy, while the Italians can do nothing without injuring their own kith and kin across the border. This dropping of explosives on the chance of hitting one soldier among fifty victims seems to me the most monstrous development of the whole war, and the one which should be most sternly repressed in future international legislation—if such a thing as international law still exists. The Italian headquarter town, which I will call Nemini, was a particular victim of these murderous attacks. I speak with some feeling, as not only was the ceiling of my bedroom shattered some days before my arrival, but a greasy patch with some black shreds upon it was still visible above my window which represented part of the remains of an unfortunate workman, who had been blown to pieces immediately in front of the house. The air defence is very skilfully managed however, and the Italians have the matter well in hand.

My first experience of the Italian line was at the portion which I have called the gap by the sea, otherwise the Isonzo front. From a mound behind the trenches an extraordinary fine view can be got of the Austrian position, the general curve of both lines being marked, as in Flanders, by the sausage balloons which float behind them. The Isonzo, which has been so bravely carried by the Italians, lay in front of me, a clear blue river, as broad as the Thames at Hampton Court. In a hollow to my left were the roofs of Gorizia, the town which the Italians are endeavouring to take. A long desolate ridge, the Carso, extends to the south of the town, and stretches down nearly to the sea. The crest is held by the Austrians and the Italian trenches have been pushed within fifty yards of them. A lively bombardment was going on from either side, but so far as the infantry goes there is none of that constant malignant petty warfare with which we are familiar in Flanders. I was anxious to see the Italian trenches, in order to compare them with our British methods, but save for the support and communication trenches I was courteously but firmly warned off.

The story of trench attack and defence is no doubt very similar in all quarters, but I am convinced that close touch should be kept between the Allies on the matter of new inventions. The quick Latin brain may conceive and test an idea long before we do. At present there seems to be very imperfect sympathy. As an example, when I was on the British lines they were dealing with a method of clearing barbed wire. The experiments were new and were causing great interest. But on the Italian front I found that the same system had been tested for many months. In the use of bullet proof jackets for engineers and other men who have to do exposed work the Italians are also ahead of us. One of their engineers at our headquarters might give some valuable advice. At present the Italians have, as I understand, no military representative with our armies, while they receive a British General with a small staff. This seems very wrong not only from the point of view of courtesy and justice, but also because Italy has no direct means of knowing the truth about our great development. When Germans state that our new armies are made of paper, our Allies should have some official assurance of their own that this is false. I can understand our keeping neutrals from our headquarters, but surely our Allies should be on another footing.

Having got this general view of the position I was anxious in the afternoon to visit Monfalcone, which is the small dockyard captured from the Austrians on the Adriatic. My kind Italian officer guides did not recommend the trip, as it was part of their great hospitality to shield their guest from any part of that danger which they were always ready to incur themselves. The only road to Monfalcone ran close to the Austrian position at the village of Ronchi, and afterwards kept parallel to it for some miles. I was told that it was only on odd days that the Austrian guns were active in this particular section, so determined to trust to luck that this might not be one of them. It proved, however, to be one of the worst on record, and we were not destined to see the dockyard to which we started.

The civilian cuts a ridiculous figure when he enlarges upon small adventures which may come his way—adventures which the soldier endures in silence as part of his everyday life. On this occasion, however, the episode was all our own, and had a sporting flavour in it which made it dramatic. I know now the feeling of tense expectation with which the driven grouse whirrs onwards towards the butt. I have been behind the butt before now, and it is only poetic justice that I should see the matter from the other point of view. As we approached Ronchi we could see shrapnel breaking over the road in front of us, but we had not yet realised that it was precisely for vehicles that the Austrians were waiting, and that they had the range marked out to a yard. We went down the road all out at a steady fifty miles an hour. The village was near, and it seemed that we had got past the place of danger. We had in fact just reached it. At this moment there was a noise as if the whole four tyres had gone simultaneously, a most terrific bang in our very ears, merging into a second sound like a reverberating blow upon an enormous gong. As I glanced up I saw three clouds immediately above my head, two of them white and the other of a rusty red. The air was full of flying metal, and the road, as we were told afterwards by an observer, was all churned up by it. The metal base of one of the shells was found plumb in the middle of the road just where our motor had been. There is no use telling me Austrian gunners can't shoot. I know better.

It was our pace that saved us. The motor was an open one, and the three shells burst, according to one of my Italian companions who was himself an artillery officer, about ten metres above our heads. They threw forward, however, and we travelling at so great a pace shot from under. Before they could get in another we had swung round the curve and under the lee of a house. The good Colonel B. wrung my hand in silence. They were both distressed, these good soldiers, under the impression that they had led me into danger. As a matter of fact it was I who owed them an apology, since they had enough risks in the way of business without taking others in order to gratify the whim of a joy-rider. Barbariche and Clericetti, this record will convey to you my remorse.

Our difficulties were by no means over. We found an ambulance lorry and a little group of infantry huddled under the same shelter with the expression of people who had been caught in the rain. The road beyond was under heavy fire as well as that by which we had come. Had the Ostro-Boches dropped a high-explosive upon us they would have had a good mixed bag. But apparently they were only out for fancy shooting and disdained a sitter. Presently there came a lull and the lorry moved on, but we soon heard a burst of firing which showed that they were after it. My companions had decided that it was out of the question for us to finish our excursion. We waited for some time therefore and were able finally to make our retreat on foot, being joined later by the car. So ended my visit to Monfalcone, the place I did not reach. I hear that two 10,000-ton steamers were left on the stocks there by the Austrians, but were disabled before they retired. Their cabin basins and other fittings are now adorning the Italian dug-outs.

My second day was devoted to a view of the Italian mountain warfare in the Carnic Alps. Besides the two great fronts, one of defence (Trentino) and one of offence (Isonzo), there are very many smaller valleys which have to be guarded. The total frontier line is over four hundred miles, and it has all to be held against raids if not invasions. It is a most picturesque business. Far up in the Roccolana Valley I found the Alpini outposts, backed by artillery which had been brought into the most wonderful positions. They have taken 8-inch guns where a tourist could hardly take his knapsack. Neither side can ever make serious progress, but there are continual duels, gun against gun, or Alpini against Jaeger. In a little wayside house was the brigade headquarters, and here I was entertained to lunch. It was a scene that I shall remember. They drank to England. I raised my glass to Italia irredenta—might it soon be redenta. They all sprang to their feet and the circle of dark faces flashed into flame. They keep their souls and emotions, these people. I trust that ours may not become atrophied by self-suppression.

The Italians are a quick high-spirited race, and it is very necessary that we should consider their feelings, and that we should show our sympathy with what they have done, instead of making querulous and unreasonable demands of them. In some ways they are in a difficult position. The war is made by their splendid king—a man of whom every one speaks with extraordinary reverence and love—and by the people. The people, with the deep instinct of a very old civilisation, understand that the liberty of the world and their own national existence are really at stake. But there are several forces which divide the strength of the nation. There is the clerical, which represents the old Guelph or German spirit, looking upon Austria as the eldest daughter of the Church—a daughter who is little credit to her mother. Then there is the old nobility. Finally, there are the commercial people who through the great banks or other similar agencies have got into the influence and employ of the Germans. When you consider all this you will appreciate how necessary it is that Britain should in every possible way, moral and material, sustain the national party. Should by any evil chance the others gain the upper hand there might be a very sudden and sinister change in the international situation. Every man who does, says, or writes a thing which may in any way alienate the Italians is really, whether he knows it or not, working for the King of Prussia. They are a grand people, striving most efficiently for the common cause, with all the dreadful disabilities which an absence of coal and iron entails. It is for us to show that we appreciate it. Justice as well as policy demands it.

The last day spent upon the Italian front was in the Trentino. From Verona a motor drive of about twenty-five miles takes one up the valley of the Adige, and past a place of evil augury for the Austrians, the field of Rivoli. As one passes up the valley one appreciates that on their left wing the Italians have position after position in the spurs of the mountains before they could be driven into the plain. If the Austrians could reach the plain it would be to their own ruin, for the Italians have large reserves. There is no need for any anxiety about the Trentino.

The attitude of the people behind the firing line should give one confidence. I had heard that the Italians were a nervous people. It does not apply to this part of Italy. As I approached the danger spot I saw rows of large, fat gentlemen with long thin black cigars leaning against walls in the sunshine. The general atmosphere would have steadied an epileptic. Italy is perfectly sure of herself in this quarter. Finally, after a long drive of winding gradients, always beside the Adige, we reached Ala, where we interviewed the Commander of the Sector, a man who has done splendid work during the recent fighting. 'By all means you can see my front. But no motorcar, please. It draws fire and others may be hit beside you.' We proceeded on foot therefore along a valley which branched at the end into two passes. In both very active fighting had been going on, and as we came up the guns were baying merrily, waking up most extraordinary echoes in the hills. It was difficult to believe that it was not thunder. There was one terrible voice that broke out from time to time in the mountains—the angry voice of the Holy Roman Empire. When it came all other sounds died down into nothing. It was—so I was told—the master gun, the vast 42 centimetre giant which brought down the pride of Liége and Namur. The Austrians have brought one or more from Innsbruck. The Italians assure me, however, as we have ourselves discovered, that in trench work beyond a certain point the size of the gun makes little matter.

We passed a burst dug-out by the roadside where a tragedy had occurred recently, for eight medical officers were killed in it by a single shell. There was no particular danger in the valley however, and the aimed fire was all going across us to the fighting lines in the two passes above us. That to the right, the Valley of Buello, has seen some of the worst of the fighting. These two passes form the Italian left wing which has held firm all through. So has the right wing. It is only the centre which has been pushed in by the concentrated fire.

When we arrived at the spot where the two valleys forked we were halted, and we were not permitted to advance to the advance trenches which lay upon the crests above us. There was about a thousand yards between the adversaries. I have seen types of some of the Bosnian and Croatian prisoners, men of poor physique and intelligence, but the Italians speak with chivalrous praise of the bravery of the Hungarians and of the Austrian Jaeger. Some of their proceedings disgust them however, and especially the fact that they use Russian prisoners to dig trenches under fire. There is no doubt of this, as some of the men were recaptured and were sent on to join their comrades in France. On the whole, however, it may be said that in the Austro-Italian war there is nothing which corresponds with the extreme bitterness of our western conflict. The presence or absence of the Hun makes all the difference.

Nothing could be more cool or methodical than the Italian arrangements on the Trentino front. There are no troops who would not have been forced back by the Austrian fire. It corresponded with the French experience at Verdun, or ours at the second battle of Ypres. It may well occur again if the Austrians get their guns forward. But at such a rate it would take them a long time to make any real impression. One cannot look at the officers and men without seeing that their spirit and confidence are high. In answer to my inquiry they assure me that there is little difference between the troops of the northern provinces and those of the south. Even among the snows of the Alps they tell me that the Sicilians gave an excellent account of themselves.

That night found me back at Verona, and next morning I was on my way to Paris, where I hope to be privileged to have some experiences at the front of our splendid Allies. I leave Italy with a deep feeling of gratitude for the kindness shown to me, and of admiration for the way in which they are playing their part in the world's fight for freedom. They have every possible disadvantage, economic and political. But in spite of it they have done splendidly. Three thousand square kilometres of the enemy's country are already in their possession. They relieve to a very great extent the pressure upon the Russians, who, in spite of all their bravery, might have been overwhelmed last summer during the 'durchbruch' had it not been for the diversion of so many Austrian troops. The time has come now when Russia by her advance on the Pripet is repaying her debt. But the debt is common to all the Allies. Let them bear it in mind. There has been mischief done by slighting criticism and by inconsiderate words. A warm sympathetic hand-grasp of congratulation is what Italy has deserved, and it is both justice and policy to give it.

A GLIMPSE OF THE FRENCH LINE

I

The French soldiers are grand. They are grand. There is no other word to express it. It is not merely their bravery. All races have shown bravery in this war. But it is their solidity, their patience, their nobility. I could not conceive anything finer than the bearing of their officers. It is proud without being arrogant, stern without being fierce, serious without being depressed. Such, too, are the men whom they lead with such skill and devotion. Under the frightful hammer-blows of circumstance, the national characters seem to have been reversed. It is our British soldier who has become debonair, light-hearted and reckless, while the Frenchman has developed a solemn stolidity and dour patience which was once all our own. During a long day in the French trenches, I have never once heard the sound of music or laughter, nor have I once seen a face that was not full of the most grim determination.

Germany set out to bleed France white. Well, she has done so. France is full of widows and orphans from end to end. Perhaps in proportion to her population she has suffered the most of all. But in carrying out her hellish mission Germany has bled herself white also. Her heavy sword has done its work, but the keen French rapier has not lost its skill. France will stand at last, weak and tottering, with her huge enemy dead at her feet. But it is a fearsome business to see—such a business as the world never looked upon before. It is fearful for the French. It is fearful for the Germans. May God's curse rest upon the arrogant men and the unholy ambitions which let loose this horror upon humanity! Seeing what they have done, and knowing that they have done it, one would think that mortal brain would grow crazy under the weight. Perhaps the central brain of all was crazy from the first. But what sort of government is it under which one crazy brain can wreck mankind!

If ever one wanders into the high places of mankind, the places whence the guidance should come, it seems to me that one has to recall the dying words of the Swedish Chancellor who declared that the folly of those who governed was what had amazed him most in his experience of life. Yesterday I met one of these men of power—M. Clemenceau, once Prime Minister, now the destroyer of governments. He is by nature a destroyer, incapable of rebuilding what he has pulled down. With his personal force, his eloquence, his thundering voice, his bitter pen, he could wreck any policy, but would not even trouble to suggest an alternative. As he sat before me with his face of an old prizefighter (he is remarkably like Jim Mace as I can remember him in his later days), his angry grey eyes and his truculent, mischievous smile, he seemed to me a very dangerous man. His conversation, if a squirt on one side and Niagara on the other can be called conversation, was directed for the moment upon the iniquity of the English rate of exchange, which seemed to me very much like railing against the barometer. My companion, who has forgotten more economics than ever Clemenceau knew, was about to ask whether France was prepared to take the rouble at face value, but the roaring voice, like a strong gramophone with a blunt needle, submerged all argument. We have our dangerous men, but we have no one in the same class as Clemenceau. Such men enrage the people who know them, alarm the people who don't, set every one by the ears, act as a healthy irritant in days of peace, and are a public danger in days of war.

But this is digression. I had set out to say something of a day's experience of the French front, though I shall write with a fuller pen when I return from the Argonne. It was for Soissons that we made, passing on the way a part of the scene of our own early operations, including the battlefield of Villers Cotteret —just such a wood as I had imagined. My companion's nephew was one of those Guards' officers whose bodies rest now in the village cemetery, with a little British Jack still flying above them. They lie together, and their grave is tended with pious care. Among the trees beside the road were other graves of soldiers, buried where they had fallen. 'So look around—and choose your ground—and take your rest.'

Soissons is a considerable wreck, though it is very far from being an Ypres. But the cathedral would, and will, make many a patriotic Frenchman weep. These savages cannot keep their hands off a beautiful church. Here, absolutely unchanged through the ages, was the spot where St. Louis had dedicated himself to the Crusade. Every stone of it was holy. And now the lovely old stained glass strews the floor, and the roof lies in a huge heap across the central aisle. A dog was climbing over it as we entered. No wonder the French fight well. Such sights would drive the mildest man to desperation. The abbé, a good priest, with a large humorous face, took us over his shattered domain. He was full of reminiscences of the German occupation of the place. One of his personal anecdotes was indeed marvellous. It was that a lady in the local ambulance had vowed to kiss the first French soldier who re-entered the town. She did so, and it proved to be her husband. The abbé is a good, kind, truthful man—but he has a humorous face.

A walk down a ruined street brings one to the opening of the trenches. There are marks upon the walls of the German occupation. 'Berlin—Paris,' with an arrow of direction, adorns one corner. At another the 76th Regiment have commemorated the fact that they were there in 1870 and again in 1914. If the Soissons folk are wise they will keep these inscriptions as a reminder to the rising generation. I can imagine, however, that their inclination will be to whitewash, fumigate, and forget.

A sudden turn among some broken walls takes one into the communication trench. Our guide is a Commandant of the Staff, a tall, thin man with hard, grey eyes and a severe face. It is the more severe towards us as I gather that he has been deluded into the belief that about one out of six of our soldiers goes to the trenches. For the moment he is not friends with the English. As we go along, however, we gradually get upon better terms, we discover a twinkle in the hard, grey eyes, and the day ends with an exchange of walking-sticks and a renewal of the Entente. May my cane grow into a marshal's baton.

A charming young artillery subaltern is our guide in that maze of trenches, and we walk and walk and walk, with a brisk exchange of compliments between the '75's' of the French and the '77's' of the Germans going on high over our heads. The trenches are boarded at the sides, and have a more permanent look than those of Flanders. Presently we meet a fine, brown-faced, upstanding boy, as keen as a razor, who commands this particular section. A little further on a helmeted captain of infantry, who is an expert sniper, joins our little party. Now we are at the very front trench. I had expected to see primeval men, bearded and shaggy. But the 'Poilus' have disappeared. The men around me were clean and dapper to a remarkable degree. I gathered, however, that they had their internal difficulties. On one board I read an old inscription, 'He is a Boche, but he is the inseparable companion of a French soldier.' Above was a rude drawing of a louse.

I am led to a cunning loop-hole, and have a glimpse through it of a little framed picture of French countryside. There are fields, a road, a sloping hill beyond with trees. Quite close, about thirty or forty yards away, was a low, red-tiled house. 'They are there,' said our guide. 'That is their outpost. We can hear them cough.' Only the guns were coughing that morning, so we heard nothing, but it was certainly wonderful to be so near to the enemy and yet in such peace. I suppose wondering visitors from Berlin are brought up also to hear the French cough. Modern warfare has certainly some extraordinary sides.

Now we are shown all the devices which a year of experience has suggested to the quick brains of our Allies. It is ground upon which one cannot talk with freedom. Every form of bomb, catapult, and trench mortar was ready to hand. Every method of cross-fire had been thought out to an exact degree. There was something, however, about their disposition of a machine gun which disturbed the Commandant. He called for the officer of the gun. His thin lips got thinner and his grey eyes more austere as we waited. Presently there emerged an extraordinarily handsome youth, dark as a Spaniard, from some rabbit hole. He faced the Commandant bravely, and answered back with respect but firmness. 'Pourquoi?' asked the Commandant, and yet again 'Pourquoi?' Adonis had an answer for everything. Both sides appealed to the big Captain of Snipers, who was clearly embarrassed. He stood on one leg and scratched his chin. Finally the Commandant turned away angrily in the midst of one of Adonis' voluble sentences. His face showed that the matter was not ended. War is taken very seriously in the French army, and any sort of professional mistake is very quickly punished. I have been told how many officers of high rank have been broken by the French during the war. The figure was a very high one. There is no more forgiveness for the beaten General than there was in the days of the Republic when the delegate of the National Convention, with a patent portable guillotine, used to drop in at headquarters to support a more vigorous offensive.

As I write these lines there is a burst of bugles in the street, and I go to my open window to see the 41st of the line march down into what may develop into a considerable battle. How I wish they could march down the Strand even as they are. How London would rise to them! Laden like donkeys, with a pile upon their backs and very often both hands full as well, they still get a swing into their march which it is good to see. They march in column of platoons, and the procession is a long one, for a French regiment is, of course, equal to three battalions. The men are shortish, very thick, burned brown in the sun, with never a smile among them—have I not said that they are going down to a grim sector?—but with faces of granite. There was a time when we talked of stiffening the French army. I am prepared to believe that our first expeditionary force was capable of stiffening any conscript army, for I do not think that a finer force ever went down to battle. But to talk about stiffening these people now would be ludicrous. You might as well stiffen the old Guard. There may be weak regiments somewhere, but I have never seen them.

I think that an injustice has been done to the French army by the insistence of artists and cinema operators upon the picturesque Colonial corps. One gets an idea that Arabs and negroes are pulling France out of the fire. It is absolutely false. Her own brave sons are doing the work. The Colonial element is really a very small one—so small that I have not seen a single unit during all my French wanderings. The Colonials are good men, but like our splendid Highlanders they catch the eye in a way which is sometimes a little hard upon their neighbours. When there is hard work to be done it is the good little French piou-piou who usually has to do it. There is no better man in Europe. If we are as good—and I believe we are—it is something to be proud of.

But I have wandered far from the trenches of Soissons. It had come on to rain heavily, and we were forced to take refuge in the dugout of the sniper. Eight of us sat in the deep gloom huddled closely together. The Commandant was still harping upon that ill-placed machine gun. He could not get over it. My imperfect ear for French could not follow all his complaints, but some defence of the offender brought forth a 'Jamais! Jamais! Jamais!' which was rapped out as if it came from the gun itself. There were eight of us in an underground burrow, and some were smoking. Better a deluge than such an atmosphere as that. But if there is a thing upon earth which the French officer shies at it is rain and mud. The reason is that he is extraordinarily natty in his person. His charming blue uniform, his facings, his brown gaiters, boots and belts are always just as smart as paint. He is the Dandy of the European war. I noticed officers in the trenches with their trousers carefully pressed. It is all to the good, I think. Wellington said that the dandies made his best officers. It is difficult for the men to get rattled or despondent when they see the debonair appearance of their leaders.

Among the many neat little marks upon the French uniforms which indicate with precision but without obtrusion the rank and arm of the wearer, there was one which puzzled me. It was to be found on the left sleeve of men of all ranks, from generals to privates, and it consisted of small gold chevrons, one, two, or more. No rule seemed to regulate them, for the general might have none, and I have heard of the private who wore ten. Then I solved the mystery.

They are the record of wounds received. What an admirable idea! Surely we should hasten to introduce it among our own soldiers. It costs little and it means much. If you can allay the smart of a wound by the knowledge that it brings lasting honour to the man among his fellows, then surely it should be done. Medals, too, are more freely distributed and with more public parade than in our service. I am convinced that the effect is good.

The rain has now stopped, and we climb from our burrow. Again we are led down that endless line of communication trench, again we stumble through the ruins, again we emerge into the street where our cars are awaiting us. Above our heads the sharp artillery duel is going merrily forward. The French are firing three or four to one, which has been my experience at every point I have touched upon the Allied front. Thanks to the extraordinary zeal of the French workers, especially of the French women, and to the clever adaptation of machinery by their engineers, their supplies are abundant. Even now they turn out more shells a day than we do. That, however, excludes our supply for the Fleet. But it is one of the miracles of the war that the French, with their coal and iron in the hands of the enemy, have been able to equal the production of our great industrial centres. The steel, of course, is supplied by us. To that extent we can claim credit for the result.

And so, after the ceremony of the walking-sticks, we bid adieu to the lines of Soissons. To-morrow we start for a longer tour to the more formidable district of the Argonne, the neighbour of Verdun, and itself the scene of so much that is glorious and tragic.

II.

There is a couplet of Stevenson's which haunts me, 'There fell a war in a woody place—in a land beyond the sea.' I have just come back from spending three wonderful dream days in that woody place. It lies with the open, bosky country of Verdun on its immediate right, and the chalk downs of Champagne upon its left. If one could imagine the lines being taken right through our New Forest or the American Adirondacks it would give some idea of the terrain, save that it is a very undulating country of abrupt hills and dales. It is this peculiarity which has made the war on this front different to any other, more picturesque and more secret. In front the fighting lines are half in the clay soil, half behind the shelter of fallen trunks. Between the two the main bulk of the soldiers live like animals of the woodlands, burrowing on the hillsides and among the roots of the trees. It is a war by itself, and a very wonderful one to see. At three different points I have visited the front in this broad region, wandering from the lines of one army corps to that of another. In all three I found the same conditions, and in all three I found also the same pleasing fact which I had discovered at Soissons, that the fire of the French was at least five, and very often ten shots to one of the Boche. It used not to be so. The Germans used to scrupulously return shot for shot. But whether they have moved their guns to the neighbouring Verdun, or whether, as is more likely, all the munitions are going there, it is certain that they were very outclassed upon the three days (June 10, 11, 12) which I allude to. There were signs that for some reason their spirits were at a low ebb. On the evening before our arrival the French had massed all their bands at the front, and, in honour of the Russian victory, had played the Marseillaise and the Russian National hymn, winding up with general shoutings and objurgations calculated to annoy. Failing to stir up the Boche, they had ended by a salute from a hundred shotted guns. After trailing their coats up and down the line they had finally to give up the attempt to draw the enemy. Want of food may possibly have caused a decline in the German spirit. There is some reason to believe that they feed up their fighting men at the places like Verdun or Hooge, where they need all their energy, at the expense of the men who are on the defensive. If so, we may find it out when we attack. The French officers assured me that the prisoners and deserters made bitter complaints of their scale of rations. And yet it is hard to believe that the fine efforts of our enemy at Verdun are the work of half-starved men.

To return to my personal impressions, it was at Chalons that we left the Paris train—a town which was just touched by the most forward ripple of the first great German floodtide. A drive of some twenty miles took us to St. Menehould, and another ten brought us to the front in the sector of Divisional-General H. A fine soldier this, and heaven help Germany if he and his division get within its borders, for he is, as one can see at a glance, a man of iron who has been goaded to fierceness by all that his beloved country has endured. He is a man of middle size, swarthy, hawk-like, very abrupt in his movements, with two steel grey eyes, which are the most searching that mine have ever met. His hospitality and courtesy to us were beyond all bounds, but there is another side to him, and it is one which it is wiser not to provoke. In person he took us to his lines, passing through the usual shot-torn villages behind them. Where the road dips down into the great forest there is one particular spot which is visible to the German artillery observers. The General mentioned it at the time, but his remark seemed to have no personal interest. We understood it better on our return in the evening.

Now we found ourselves in the depths of the woods, primeval woods of oak and beech in the deep clay soil that the great oak loves. There had been rain and the forest paths were ankle deep in mire. Everywhere, to right and left, soldiers' faces, hard and rough from a year of open air, gazed up at us from their burrows in the ground. Presently an alert, blue-clad figure stood in the path to greet us. It was the Colonel of the sector. He was ridiculously like Cyrano de Bergerac as depicted by the late M. Coquelin, save that his nose was of more moderate proportion. The ruddy colouring, the bristling feline full-ended moustache, the solidity of pose, the backward tilt of the head, the general suggestion of the bantam cock, were all there facing us as he stood amid the leaves in the sunlight. Gauntlets and a long rapier—nothing else was wanting. Something had amused Cyrano. His moustache quivered with suppressed mirth, and his blue eyes were demurely gleaming. Then the joke came out. He had spotted a German working party, his guns had concentrated on it, and afterwards he had seen the stretchers go forward. A grim joke, it may seem. But the French see this war from a different angle to us. If we had the Boche sitting on our heads for two years, and were not yet quite sure whether we could ever get him off again, we should get Cyrano's point of view. Those of us who have had our folk murdered by Zeppelins or tortured in German prisons have probably got it already.

We passed in a little procession among the French soldiers, and viewed their multifarious arrangements. For them we were a little break in a monotonous life, and they formed up in lines as we passed. My own British uniform and the civilian dresses of my two companions interested them. As the General passed these groups, who formed themselves up in perhaps a more familiar manner than would have been usual in the British service, he glanced kindly at them with those singular eyes of his, and once or twice addressed them as 'Mes enfants.' One might conceive that all was 'go as you please' among the French. So it is as long as you go in the right way. When you stray from it you know it. As we passed a group of men standing on a low ridge which overlooked us there was a sudden stop. I gazed round. The General's face was steel and cement. The eyes were cold and yet fiery, sunlight upon icicles. Something had happened. Cyrano had sprung to his side. His reddish moustache had shot forward beyond his nose, and it bristled out like that of an angry cat. Both were looking up at the group above us. One wretched man detached himself from his comrades and sidled down the slope. No skipper and mate of a Yankee blood boat could have looked more ferociously at a mutineer. And yet it was all over some minor breach of discipline which was summarily disposed of by two days of confinement. Then in an instant the faces relaxed, there was a general buzz of relief and we were back at 'Mes enfants' again. But don't make any mistake as to discipline in the French army.

Trenches are trenches, and the main specialty of these in the Argonne is that they are nearer to the enemy. In fact there are places where they interlock, and where the advanced posts lie cheek by jowl with a good steel plate to cover both cheek and jowl. We were brought to a sap-head where the Germans were at the other side of a narrow forest road. Had I leaned forward with extended hand and a Boche done the same we could have touched. I looked across, but saw only a tangle of wire and sticks. Even whispering was not permitted in these forward posts.

When we emerged from these hushed places of danger Cyrano took us all to his dug-out, which was a tasty little cottage carved from the side of a hill and faced with logs. He did the honours of the humble cabin with the air of a seigneur in his château. There was little furniture, but from some broken mansion he had extracted an iron fire-back, which adorned his grate. It was a fine, mediaeval bit of work, with Venus, in her traditional costume, in the centre of it. It seemed the last touch in the picture of the gallant, virile Cyrano. I only met him this once, nor shall I ever see him again, yet he stands a thing complete within my memory. Even now as I write these lines he walks the leafy paths of the Argonne, his fierce eyes ever searching for the Boche workers, his red moustache bristling over their annihilation. He seems a figure out of the past of France.

That night we dined with yet another type of the French soldier, General A., who commands the corps of which my friend has one division. Each of these French generals has a striking individuality of his own which I wish I could fix upon paper. Their only common point is that each seems to be a rare good soldier. The corps general is Athos with a touch of d'Artagnan. He is well over six feet high, bluff, jovial, with huge, up-curling moustache, and a voice that would rally a regiment. It is a grand figure which should have been done by Van Dyck with lace collar, hand on sword, and arm akimbo. Jovial and laughing was he, but a stern and hard soldier was lurking behind the smiles. His name may appear in history, and so may Humbert's, who rules all the army of which the other's corps is a unit. Humbert is a Lord Robert's figure, small, wiry, quick-stepping, all steel and elastic, with a short, sharp upturned moustache, which one could imagine as crackling with electricity in moments of excitement like a cat's fur. What he does or says is quick, abrupt, and to the point. He fires his remarks like pistol shots at this man or that. Once to my horror he fixed me with his hard little eyes and demanded 'Sherlock Holmes, est ce qu'il est un soldat dans l'armée Anglaise?' The whole table waited in an awful hush. 'Mais, mon general,' I stammered, 'il est trop vieux pour service.' There was general laughter, and I felt that I had scrambled out of an awkward place.

And talking of awkward places, I had forgotten about that spot upon the road whence the Boche observer could see our motor-cars. He had actually laid a gun upon it, the rascal, and waited all the long day for our return. No sooner did we appear upon the slope than a shrapnel shell burst above us, but somewhat behind me, as well as to the left. Had it been straight the second car would have got it, and there might have been a vacancy in one of the chief editorial chairs in London. The General shouted to the driver to speed up, and we were soon safe from the German gunners. One gets perfectly immune to noises in these scenes, for the guns which surround you make louder crashes than any shell which bursts about you. It is only when you actually see the cloud over you that your thoughts come back to yourself, and that you realise that in this wonderful drama you may be a useless super, but none the less you are on the stage and not in the stalls.

Next morning we were down in the front trenches again at another portion of the line. Far away on our right, from a spot named the Observatory, we could see the extreme left of the Verdun position and shells bursting on the Fille Morte. To the north of us was a broad expanse of sunny France, nestling villages, scattered châteaux, rustic churches, and all as inaccessible as if it were the moon. It is a terrible thing this German bar—a thing unthinkable to Britons. To stand on the edge of Yorkshire and look into Lancashire feeling that it is in other hands, that our fellow-countrymen are suffering there and waiting, waiting, for help, and that we cannot, after two years, come a yard nearer to them—would it not break our hearts? Can I wonder that there is no smile upon the grim faces of these Frenchmen! But when the bar is broken, when the line sweeps forward, as most surely it will, when French bayonets gleam on yonder uplands and French flags break from those village spires— ah, what a day that will be! Men will die that day from the pure, delirious joy of it. We cannot think what it means to France, and the less so because she stands so nobly patient waiting for her hour.

Yet another type of French general takes us round this morning! He, too, is a man apart, an unforgettable man. Conceive a man with a large broad good-humoured face, and two placid, dark seal's eyes which gaze gently into yours. He is young and has pink cheeks and a soft voice. Such is one of the most redoubtable fighters of France, this General of Division D. His former staff officers told me something of the man. He is a philosopher, a fatalist, impervious to fear, a dreamer of distant dreams amid the most furious bombardment. The weight of the French assault upon the terrible labyrinth fell at one time upon the brigade which he then commanded. He led them day after day gathering up Germans with the detached air of the man of science who is hunting for specimens. In whatever shell-hole he might chance to lunch he had his cloth spread and decorated with wild flowers plucked from the edge. If fate be kind to him he will go far. Apart from his valour he is admitted to be one of the most scientific soldiers of France.

From the Observatory we saw the destruction of a German trench. There had been signs of work upon it, so it was decided to close it down. It was a very visible brown streak a thousand yards away. The word was passed back to the '75's' in the rear. There was a 'tir rapide' over our heads. My word, the man who stands fast under a 'tir rapide,' be he Boche, French or British, is a man of mettle! The mere passage of the shells was awe-inspiring, at first like the screaming of a wintry wind, and then thickening into the howling of a pack of wolves. The trench was a line of terrific explosions. Then the dust settled down and all was still. Where were the ants who had made the nest? Were they buried beneath it? Or had they got from under? No one could say.

There was one little gun which fascinated me, and I stood for some time watching it. Its three gunners, enormous helmeted men, evidently loved it, and touched it with a swift but tender touch in every movement. When it was fired it ran up an inclined plane to take off the recoil, rushing up and then turning and rattling down again upon the gunners who were used to its ways. The first time it did it, I was standing behind it, and I don't know which moved quickest —the gun or I.

French officers above a certain rank develop and show their own individuality. In the lower grades the conditions of service enforce a certain uniformity. The British officer is a British gentleman first, and an officer afterwards. The Frenchman is an officer first, though none the less the gentleman stands behind it. One very strange type we met, however, in these Argonne Woods. He was a French-Canadian who had been a French soldier, had founded a homestead in far Alberta, and had now come back of his own will, though a naturalised Briton, to the old flag. He spoke English of a kind, the quality and quantity being equally extraordinary. It poured from him and was, so far as it was intelligible, of the woolly Western variety. His views on the Germans were the most emphatic we had met. 'These Godam sons of'—well, let us say 'Canines!' he would shriek, shaking his fist at the woods to the north of him. A good man was our compatriot, for he had a very recent Legion of Honour pinned upon his breast. He had been put with a few men on Hill 285, a sort of volcano stuffed with mines, and was told to telephone when he needed relief. He refused to telephone and remained there for three weeks. 'We sit like a rabbit in his hall,' he explained. He had only one grievance. There were many wild boars in the forest, but the infantry were too busy to get them. 'The Godam Artillaree he get the wild pig!' Out of his pocket he pulled a picture of a frame-house with snow round it, and a lady with two children on the stoop. It was his homestead at Trochu, seventy miles north of Calgary.

It was the evening of the third day that we turned our faces to Paris once more. It was my last view of the French. The roar of their guns went far with me upon my way. Soldiers of France, farewell! In your own phrase I salute you! Many have seen you who had more knowledge by which to judge your manifold virtues, many also who had more skill to draw you as you are, but never one, I am sure, who admired you more than I. Great was the French soldier under Louis the Sun-King, great too under Napoleon, but never was he greater than to-day.

And so it is back to England and to home. I feel sobered and solemn from all that I have seen. It is a blind vision which does not see more than the men and the guns, which does not catch something of the terrific spiritual conflict which is at the heart of it.

  Mine eyes have seen the glory of the coming of the Lord

  —He is trampling out the vineyard where the grapes of wrath are stored.

We have found no inspired singer yet, like Julia Howe, to voice the divine meaning of it all—that meaning which is more than numbers or guns upon the day of battle. But who can see the adult manhood of Europe standing in a double line, waiting for a signal to throw themselves upon each other, without knowing that he has looked upon the most terrific of all the dealings between the creature below and that great force above, which works so strangely towards some distant but glorious end?